SUNSHINE'S TANGLED TRESSES

By: La-Shonda Rice

Dedication

To my loving husband and best friend, Vernon: Because you believed in me; it has kept me inspired and focused.

To Brazil, my sun (son): Your laughter, smile, and confidence warms my heart. My dear Prince, please forgive me for the nights that you wanted to sleep in my bed while Daddy was at work and I told you no. This is what Mommy was doing.

To Genesis, my cupcake: You are the inspiration for this book. The day that you came to me and told me you didn't like your hair, it broke my heart. It made me think I failed you. That was the beginning of us celebrating you more and educating you on the history of black hair. Always remember, when you look in that mirror, to appreciate every feature - every kink and curl because you are worthy of being celebrated every day! YOU ARE PERFECTLY PERFECT!

To every Queen in training: God made no mistakes. Adjust your crown and know that you are beautiful.

To every family member and friend that went into action after I shared with you how Cupcake felt about her hair: You protected my daughter's self-esteem. As a team, we showered her with love and made her proud of her beautiful hair. I can't thank you enough.

To You: Yes, you reading this. Thank you for your support. I am grateful you have selected this book over millions of others. May the good Lord bless you. This is only the beginning.

"Sunshine, it's time to get ready for church," mom yelled to Sunshine from the kitchen downstairs.

Sunshine was hiding under the covers. She was used to the Sunday routine. She had to brush her teeth, wash her face, make her bed, have breakfast with the family, and then came the part she always dreaded. Mom had to do her hair.

Sunshine didn't like her hair. It was too thick, too fluffy, too tangled and too dark. She looked in her vanity and stared at her giant, untamed puff.

"Sunshine, let's go honey. We are going to be late," mom said. But Sunshine continued to move like pond water, without a care.

Why couldn't her hair be like her classmate Melissa's hair? Her hair was long, brown, and wavy. It was so wavy it looked like a calm ocean somewhere off an island under the moonlight.

Or, how about that rock star on television? She has cool, pink hair with big loose curls all around her face. Who wouldn't want hair like that? Sunshine thought.

Maybe if her hair was long, straight, and blonde like Rapunzel? "Oh yes, she thought. She could put it in one long braid." Everyone would applaud and say, "Sunshine, your hair is so amazingly golden. Sunshine, how do you get your hair so long? Sunshine, who styles your hair?" While cameras flashed all around her, she imagined herself responding in a posh tone saying, "it is exclusive information, darling."

As she looked in the mirror and sighed at her tangled tresses - she thought, "but none of that is real." It wasn't straight, it wasn't very long and it definitely wasn't blonde.

Sunshine headed downstairs before her mom called for the third time. She knew if mom had to call her again, she would be on her way upstairs and she didn't want that.

During breakfast, Sunshine ate her food very slowly. She picked at her eggs, nibbled her toast like a mouse, and sipped her orange juice very slowly. She was hoping that they would be running so late she could just wear a hat to church. That way no one would see her hair at all. Everyone would give her the head nod of approval at her fancy, white, straw hat with the big, yellow sunflower to match her dress.

"Alright, honey! You have stalled long enough," Mom said. Mom instructed her to go get the comb, brush, grease, the spray bottle with water, and hair supply basket. Momma was too sharp. She knew Sunshine was trying to wear her beat up straw hat to avoid her hair being styled.

Sunshine stomped her way upstairs and noticed her favorite dress was stretched across her bed. It was white with a cow patch print and sunflowers on the front. Granny bought it last year. At first, it was too big but Sunshine quickly grew into it. Now it fits just right. "Well at least I get to wear my favorite dress," said Sunshine.

Sunshine came down the stairs just as slowly as she walked up them. She placed all the items her mom asked for on the floor near her mother's feet. She then plopped down between her mother's legs and asked, "Momma, how come my hair isn't straight?"

"Well, baby .... because my hair isn't straight and you are a part of me." Sunshine folded her arms in disgust and said, "I don't like my hair!"

"Why don't you like your hair sweetie," asked Mom. "Because it is too tangled, too short, too dark, and too thick," said Sunshine. Mom was shocked to hear such words coming from her daughter.

She took a deep breath and said ...
"Did you know a long, long, long time ago when our people were in Africa, you could identify things about them according to their hair?"
"Really?" said Sunshine. Yes, certain styles told their age, tribe, wealth, if they were married and so much more.

Our hair is an expression of our culture. As time progressed, our hair has changed so much. In the 1970's, our people wore their hair in an afro. This was the beginning of the Black Power Movement. No matter where you went, if you saw someone with an afro, during that time, you knew they supported equality and black pride. We greeted each other by throwing our right fist in the air with our afros big and fluffy.

Years later, our hair changed again. More people were getting relaxers and putting other chemicals in their hair as an effort to change their hair texture and color. I have to be honest with you, baby, it looked really nice at first. But, Sunshine, it caused our hair to become so weak and brittle. Our hair was shedding like leaves falling from the trees in Fall. Some people's hair was so damaged they had to cut all their hair off to start all over.

"You mean some women went bald?" Sunshine asked. "Yes! Or, really short," Mom said. It had to be done in order for healthy hair to grow.

Sweetie, I want you to understand something. You are beautiful just the way God made you. From the crown of your head to the soles of your feet, you are one-of-a-kind. When you are older and you decide that you want to change your hair, it is fine.

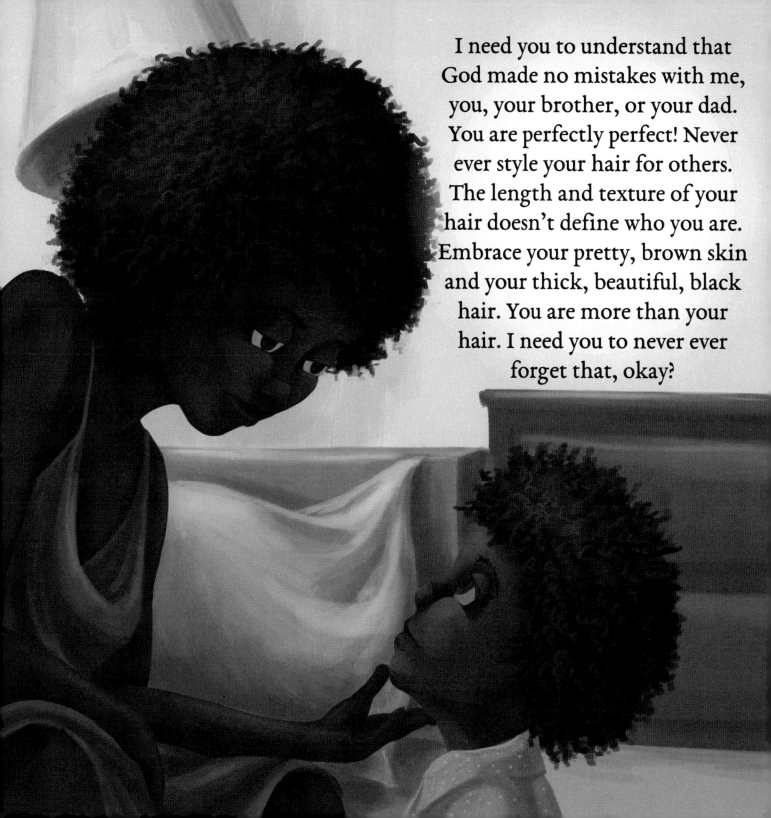

I need you to understand that
God made no mistakes with me,
you, your brother, or your dad.
You are perfectly perfect! Never
ever style your hair for others.
The length and texture of your
hair doesn't define who you are.
Embrace your pretty, brown skin
and your thick, beautiful, black
hair. You are more than your
hair. I need you to never ever
forget that, okay?

"Yes ma'am," said Sunshine. "Can you tell me a few things you like about yourself?" asked Mom. I like that I can draw really good. I like the way I dress myself. I like that I can read and do math well.

That's great, Sunshine. But, do you know what I like about you? Sunshine shakes her head no. I like your smile. I like that you are always so helpful. I like that you are funny. I like that you are kind to your brother. I like your warm hugs and kisses when I come home from work. I like the fact that you look like me, too! More importantly, I love your beautiful, brown skin and thick hair.

Sunshine hugs her mom and says, "thank you, momma. I love you so much!" Mom replied, "I love you more, honey. Do you now understand why you should embrace what you have and love everything about you?"

"Yes ma'am," said Sunshine. "Well, let's start this hair. Shall we? What style would you like it to be?" Sunshine shouted with excitement, "May I have an afro like Angela Davis?" "Why certainly," said Mom.

After Sunshine's hair was done, she put on her green, sparkly headband with a sunflower on the side. She wore medium-sized twists into an afro. It was so shiny and fluffy. Sunshine looked in her vanity mirror. This time, she imagined herself walking down a red carpet with lights flashing. People were asking her, "Sunshine, who styles your hair? Sunshine, what products do you use? Sunshine, how do you keep your hair so healthy?" She responds by saying, "I get it from my momma."

About the Author

La-Shonda Rice, aka Mrs. Lala, is the owner and doll designer of The Christian Crochet Addict, a one of a kind crochet doll company. She began her crochet experience in 1992 with a small skein of yarn and a pencil! She fell in love with all baby items, from booties, to hats, and blankets!

When people first meet Mrs. Lala, most of them are surprised to discover she was in the US ARMY and a retired New York City Police Officer. When not crocheting and writing, Mrs. Lala graces the stage acting in local plays through-out New York City. Her sense of humor, giving heart, and ability to motivate others have made her a sought-after Master of Ceremony and Motivational Speaker. She became the self designated Chaplin at her precinct by praying for her co-workers as well as all prisoners. Her creativity can be seen world-wide through her amazing one of a kind crochet baby items and dolls. La-Shonda also donates her time as a member of the Women's Industrial Service League, Inc. Providing various services for residents in her community. While recognizing senior citizens that volunteer as well as graduating scholars with yearly scholarships.

After serving in the United States Army, teaching kindergarten, working with the New York State Assembly, retiring from the New York City Police Department, and becoming a crochet doll designer, La-Shonda is excited to launch her first children's book.

La-Shonda's goal is to encourage our youth before the media or society tell them they are too fat, too skinny, their hair is too nappy, too straight, skin is too light or too dark with one book at a time.

When not crocheting, Mrs. Lala enjoys traveling with her husband, 7 year old son, and 5 year old daughter.

If you would like to know more about La-Shonda Rice and her crochet dolls, visit her website and other social media outlets below.

Website
http://www.thechristiancrochetaddict.com
Facebook
https://www.facebook.com/thechristiancrochetaddict/
Instagram
www.instagram.com/thechristiancrochetaddict
Etsy
http://etsy.me/2nshBT6

22739782R00020